The
Chase

The Kutenai Indians originally lived in the plateau region of the Northwest—now Washington, Idaho, and British Columbia. They were seminomadic, living much of the year in villages and traveling during the summer months to hunt buffalo and other game. The Kutenai were a peaceful people for whom the land and the natural world were sacred. Although they had long been friends with the white man, most were moved to reservations in Montana and Idaho during the 1890s. Today about four thousand Kutenai live in small groups on their old land.

Translation copyright © 1991 by Crown Publishers, Inc. All rights reserved. No part of this book may be reproduced or transmitted in any form or by any means, electronic or mechanical, including photocopying, recording, or by any information storage and retrieval system, without permission in writing from the publisher. Published in the United States in 1991 by Crown Publishers, Inc., a Random House company, 225 Park Avenue South, New York, NY 10003. Originally published in France in 1990 by Kaléidoscope, Paris. Copyright © 1990 by Kaléidoscope, Paris. CROWN is a trademark of Crown Publishers, Inc. Manufactured in the United States of America

Library of Congress Cataloging-in-Publication Data

Tanaka, Béatrice.
  [Course. English]
  The chase : a retelling of a Kutenai Indian tale / Béatrice Tanaka; illustrated by Michel Gay.
      p.   cm.
  Translation of: La course.
    Summary: When Coyote sees Rabbit running through the forest, he runs after Rabbit, and soon all the animals in the forest are running away.
      1. Kutenai Indians—Legends. [1. Kutenai Indians—Legends. 2. Indians of North America—Legends. 3. Animals—Folklore.] I. Gay, Michel, ill. II. Title.
E99.K85T3613   1991
398—dc20
[.2'089973]   91-10790
ISBN 0-517-58623-1 (trade)
      0-517-58624-X (lib. bdg.)

                    10 9 8 7 6 5 4 3 2 1   First American Edition

The Chase

A Kutenai Indian Tale

Told by Béatrice Tanaka

Illustrated by
Michel Gay

CROWN PUBLISHERS, INC.
New York

Coyote was sitting peacefully in the meadow when he saw Rabbit run past, quick as an arrow.

"If Rabbit's running that fast, there must be hunters after him," Coyote said to himself. "I'd better run too."

Moose, who was quietly grazing in the swamp, noticed her two friends running by.

"If Coyote's running that fast, the river must be flooding," Moose said to herself. "I'd better be off too."

Wolf, who had been lazily napping in his den, was awakened by the galloping footsteps of the three runners.

"If Moose is running that fast, the forest must be on fire," said Wolf to himself. "I'd better put off my nap until later."

Bear, who was calmly fishing in the stream, saw the four runners racing by at top speed. He recognized his friend Wolf.

"If Wolf is running that fast, the situation must be serious, very serious," thought Bear, and he lumbered off after them.

After running a good while, Bear caught up with Wolf, who was crouched in a clearing, exhausted and panting.

"What's going on?" demanded Bear. "I know someone as brave as you wouldn't run unless there was real danger."

"I have no idea," said Wolf. "It's Moose we should ask. When I saw her running so fast, I decided I'd better put off my nap and follow her."

"Tell us, Moose, why were you running?"

"I have no idea," said Moose. "It's Coyote we should ask. When I saw him run by so fast, I thought I'd better be off too."

"Say, Coyote, why were you running?"

"I have no idea," said Coyote. "It's Rabbit we should ask. When I saw how fast he was running, I thought I'd better run too. When he stopped, so did I. He'll know what terrible danger we've escaped."

"Hey, Rabbit!" cried Bear, Wolf, Moose, and Coyote together. "Why were we running?"

"Why were *you* running?" said Rabbit.
"I have no idea. But *me*—I was late for dinner!"